The Code of Honor

John Lyde Wilson

Contents

THE CODE OF HONOR

BY

John Lyde Wilson

THE CODE OF HONOR;

or

RULES FOR THE GOVERNMENT

of

PRINCIPALS AND SECONDS

in

DUELLING

by John Lyde Wilson

Summary:

Originally this was published by the author (1784-1849), a
former governor of South Carolina, as a 22-page booklet, in 1838. Before
his death he added an appendix of the 1777 Irish duelling code, but
this second edition was not printed until 1858, as a 46-page small book,
still sized to fit in the case with one's duelling pistols. This code
is far less blood-thirsty than many might suppose, but built on a closed
social caste and standards of behavior quite alien to today.

Transcriber's Note: In the appendix the term "rencontre" is used. In British law (then covering Ireland) this refers to an immediate fight in the heat of offense. A duel would be undertaken in "cold blood" if not cool temper. Killing a man in a rencontre counted as manslaughter; in a duel, as murder.

On more than one occasion, the author refers to "posting" an offender. This refers to posting to the public a notice as to his behavior in some central club or business spot frequented by all men of that level of society; exactly where varied from town to town. It was the ultimate sanction, making the challengee's refusal to either apologize or fight a public stain upon his character.

TO THE PUBLIC

The man who adds in any way to the sum of human happiness is strictly in the discharge of a moral duty. When Howard visited the victims of crime and licentiousness, to reform their habits and ameliorate their condition, the question was never asked whether he had been guilty of like excesses or not? The only question the philanthropist would propound, should be, has the deed been done in the true spirit of Christian benevolence? Those who know me, can well attest the motive which has caused the publication of the following sheets, to which they for a long time urged me in vain. Those who do not know me, have no right to impute a wrong motive; and if they do, I had rather be the object, than the authors of condemnation. To publish a CODE OF HONOR, to govern in cases of individual combat, might seem to imply, that the publisher was an advocate of duelling, and wished to introduce it as the proper mode of deciding all personal difficulties and misunderstandings.

Such implication would do me great injustice. But if the question be directly put to me, whether there are not cases where duels are right and proper, I would unhesitatingly answer, there are. If an oppressed nation has a right to appeal to arms in defence of its liberty and the happiness of its people, there can be no argument used in support of such appeal, which will not apply with equal force to individuals. How many cases are there, that might be enumerated, where there is no tribunal to do justice to an oppressed and deeply wronged individual? If he be subjected to a tame submission to insult and disgrace, where no power can shield him from its effects, then indeed it would seem, that the first law of nature, self-preservation, points out the only remedy for his wrongs. The history of all animated nature exhibits a determined resistance to encroachments upon natural rights,--nay, I might add, inanimate nature, for it also exhibits a continual warfare for supremacy. Plants of the same kind, as well as trees, do not stop their vigorous growth because they overshadow their kind; but, on the contrary, flourish with greater vigor as the more weak and delicate decline and die. Those of different species are at perpetual warfare. The sweetest rose tree will sicken and waste on the near approach of the noxious bramble, and the most promising fields of wheat yield a miserable harvest if choked up with tares and thistles. The elements themselves war together, and the angels of heaven have met in fierce encounter. The principle of self-preservation is co-extensive with creation; and when by education we make character and moral worth a part of ourselves, we guard these possessions with more watchful zeal than life itself, and would go farther for their protection. When one finds himself avoided in society, his friends shunning his approach, his substance wasting, his wife and children in want around him, and traces all his misfortunes and misery to the slanderous tongue of the calumniator, who, by secret whisper or artful innuendo, has sapped and undermined his reputation, he must be more or less than man to submit in silence.

The indiscriminate and frequent appeal to arms, to settle trivial disputes and misunderstandings, cannot be too severely censured and deprecated. I am no advocate of such duelling. But in cases where the laws of the country give no redress for injuries received, where public opinion not only authorizes, but enjoins resistance, it is needless and a waste of time to denounce the practice. It will be persisted in as long as a manly independence, and a lofty personal pride in all that dignifies and ennobles the human character, shall continue to exist. If a man be smote on one cheek in public, and he turns the other, which is also smitten, and he offers no resistance, but blesses him that so despitefully used him, I am aware that he is in the exercise of great Christian forbearance, highly recommended and enjoined by many very good men, but utterly repugnant to those feelings which nature and education have implanted in the human character. If it was possible to enact laws so severe and impossible to be evaded, as to enforce such rule of behavior, all that is honorable in the community would quit the country and inhabit the wilderness with the Indians. If such a course of conduct was infused by education into the minds of our youth, and it became praiseworthy and honorable to a man to submit to insult and indignity, then indeed the forbearance might be borne without disgrace. Those, therefore, who condemn all who do not denounce duelling in every case, should establish schools where a passive submission to force would be the exercise of a commendable virtue. I have not the least doubt, that if I had been educated in such a school, and lived in such a society, I would have proved a very good member of it. But I much doubt, if a seminary of learning was established, where this Christian forbearance was inculcated and enforced, whether there would be many scholars.

I would not wish to be understood to say, that I do not desire to see duelling to cease to exist entirely, in society. But my plan for doing it away, is essentially different from the one which teaches a passive forbearance to insult and indignity. I would inculcate in the rising generation a spirit of lofty independence; I would have them taught that nothing was more derogatory to the honor of a gentleman, than to wound the feelings of any one, however humble. That if wrong be done to another, it was more an act of heroism and bravery to repair the injury, than to persist in error, and enter into mortal combat with the injured party. This would be an aggravation of that which was already odious, and would put him without the pale of all decent society and honorable men. I would strongly inculcate the propriety of being tender of the feelings, as well as the failings, of those around him. I would teach immutable integrity, and uniform urbanity of manners. Scrupulously to guard individual honor, by a high personal self respect, and the practice of every commendable virtue. Once let such a system of education be universal, and we should seldom hear, if ever, of any more duelling.

The severest penal enactments cannot restrain the practice of duelling, and their extreme severity in this State, the more effectually shields the offenders. The teaching and preaching of our eloquent Clergy, may do some service, but is wholly inadequate to suppress it. Under these circumstances, the following rules are given to the public, and if I can save the life of one useful member of society, I will be compensated. I have restored to the bosoms of many, their sons, by my timely interference, who are ignorant of the misery I have averted from them. I believe that nine duels out of ten, if not ninety-nine out of a hundred, originate in the want of experience in the seconds. A book of authority, to which they can refer in matters where they are uninformed, will therefore be a desideratum. How far this code will be that book, the public will decide.

THE AUTHOR

RULES FOR PRINCIPALS AND SECONDS IN DUELLING.

CHAPTER I. The Person Insulted, Before Challenge Sent

1. Whenever you believe that you are insulted, if the insult be in public and by words or behavior, never resent it there, if you have self-command enough to avoid noticing it. If resented there, you offer an indignity to the company, which you should not.

2. If the insult be by blows or any personal indignity, it may be resented at the moment, for the insult to the company did not originate with you. But although resented at the moment, you are bound still to have satisfaction, and must therefore make the demand.

3. When you believe yourself aggrieved, be silent on the subject, speak to no one about the matter, and see your friend, who is to act for you, as soon as possible.

4. Never send a challenge in the first instance, for that precludes all negotiation. Let your note be in the language of a gentleman, and let the subject matter of complaint be truly and fairly set forth, cautiously avoiding attributing to the adverse party any improper motive.

5. When your second is in full possession of the facts, leave the whole matter to his judgment, and avoid any consultation with him unless he seeks it. He has the custody of your honor, and by obeying him you

cannot be compromitted.

6. Let the time of demand upon your adversary after the insult, be as short as possible, for he has the right to double that time in replying to you, unless you give him some good reason for your delay. Each party is entitled to reasonable time, to make the necessary domestic arrangements, by will or otherwise, before fighting.

7. To a written communication you are entitled to a written reply, and it is the business of your friend to require it.

SECOND'S DUTY BEFORE CHALLENGE SENT.

1. Whenever you are applied to by a friend to act as his second, before you agree to do so, state distinctly to your principal that you will be governed only by your own judgment,--that he will not be consulted after you are in full possession of the facts, unless it becomes necessary to make or accept the amende honorable, or send a challenge. You are supposed to be cool and collected, and your friend's feelings are more or less irritated.

2. Use every effort to soothe and tranquilize your principal; do not see things in the same aggravated light in which he views them; extenuate the conduct of his adversary whenever you see clearly an opportunity to do so, without doing violence to your friend's irritated mind. Endeavor to persuade him that there must have been some misunderstanding in the matter. Check him if he uses opprobrious epithet towards his adversary, and never permit improper or insulting words in the note you carry.

3. To the note you carry in writing to the party complained of, you are entitled to a written answer, which will be directed to your principal and will be delivered to you by his adversary's friend. If this be not

written in the style of a gentleman, refuse to receive it, and assign your reason for such refusal. If there be a question made as to the character of the note, require the second presenting it to you, who considers it respectful, to endorse upon it these words: "I consider the note of my friend respectful, and would not have been the bearer of it, if I believed otherwise."

4. If the party called on, refuses to receive the note you bear, you are entitled to demand a reason for such refusal. If he refuses to give you any reason, and persists in such refusal, he treats, not only your friend, but yourself, with indignity, and you must then make yourself the actor, by sending a respectful note, requiring a proper explanation of the course he has pursued towards you and your friend; and if he still adheres to his determination, you are to challenge or post him.

5. If the person to whom you deliver the note of your friend, declines meeting him on the ground of inequality, you are bound to tender yourself in his stead, by a note directed to him from yourself; and if he refuses to meet you, you are to post him.

6. In all cases of the substitution of the second for the principal, the seconds should interpose and adjust the matter, if the party substituting avows he does not make the quarrel of his principal his own. The true reason for substitution, is the supposed insult of imputing to you the like inequality which if charged upon your friend, and when the contrary is declared, there should be no fight, for individuals may well differ in their estimate of an individual's character and standing in society. In case of substitution and a satisfactory arrangement, you are then to inform your friend of all the facts, whose duty it will be to post in person.

7. If the party, to whom you present a note, employ a son, father or brother, as a second, you may decline acting with either on the ground

of consanguinity.

8. If a minor wishes you to take a note to an adult, decline doing so, on the ground of his minority. But if the adult complained of, had made a companion of the minor in society, you may bear the note.

9. When an accommodation is tendered, never require too much; and if the party offering the amende honorable, wishes to give a reason for his conduct in the matter, do not, unless offensive to your friend, refuse to receive it; by so doing you may heal the breach more effectually.

10. If a stranger wishes you to bear a note for him, be well satisfied before you do so, that he is on an equality with you; and in presenting the note state to the party the relationship you stand towards him, and what you know and believe about him; for strangers are entitled to redress for wrongs, as well as others, and the rules of honor and hospitality should protect him.

CHAPTER II. The Party Receiving a Note Before Challenge.

1. When a note is presented to you by an equal, receive it, and read it, although you may suppose it to be from one you do not intend to meet, because its requisites may be of a character which may readily be complied with. But if the requirements of a note cannot be acceded to, return it, through the medium of your friend, to the person who handed it to you, with your reason for returning it.

2. If the note received be in abusive terms, object to its reception,

and return it for that reason; but if it be respectful, return an answer of the same character, in which respond correctly and openly to all interrogatories fairly propounded, and hand it to your friend, who, it is presumed, you have consulted, and who has advised the answer; direct it to the opposite party, and let it be delivered to his friend.

3. You may refuse to receive a note, from a minor, (if you have not made an associate of him); one that has been posted; one that has been publicly disgraced without resenting it; one whose occupation is unlawful; a man in his dotage and a lunatic. There may be other cases, but the character of those enumerated will lead to a correct decision upon those omitted.

If you receive a note from a stranger, you have a right to a reasonable time to ascertain his standing in society, unless he is fully vouched for by his friend.

4. If a party delays calling on you for a week or more, after the supposed insult, and assigns no cause for the delay, if you require it, you may double the time before you respond to him; for the wrong cannot be considered aggravated; if borne patiently for some days, and the time may have been used in preparation and practice.

Second's Duty of the Party Receiving a Note Before Challenge Sent.

1. When consulted by your friend, who has received a note requiring explanation, inform him distinctly that he must be governed wholly by you in the progress of the dispute. If he refuses, decline to act on that ground.

2. Use your utmost efforts to allay all excitement which your principal may labor under; search diligently into the origin of the misunderstanding; for gentlemen seldom insult each other, unless

they labor under some misapprehension or mistake; and when you have discovered the original ground or error, follow each movement to the time of sending the note, and harmony will be restored.

3. When your principal refuses to do what you require of hi, decline further acting on that ground, and inform the opposing second of your withdrawal from the negotiation.

CHAPTER III. Duty of Challenger and His Second Before Fighting.

1. After all efforts for a reconciliation are over, the party aggrieved sends a challenge to his adversary, which is delivered to his second.

2. Upon the acceptance of the challenge, the seconds make the necessary arrangements for the meeting, in which each party is entitled to a perfect equality. The old notion that the party challenged, was authorized to name the time, place, distance and weapon, has been long since exploded; nor would a man of chivalric honor use such a right, if he possessed it. The time must e as soon as practicable, the place such as had ordinarily been used where the parties are, the distance usual, and the weapons that which is most generally used, which, in this State, is the pistol.

3. If the challengee insist upon what is not usual in time, place, distance and weapon, do not yield the point, and tender in writing what is usual in each, and if he refuses to give satisfaction, then your friend may post him.

4. If your friend be determined to fight and not post, you have the right to withdraw. But if you continue to act, and have the right to tender a still more deadly distance and weapon, and he must accept.

5. The usual distance is from ten to twenty paces, as may be agreed on; and the seconds in measuring the ground, usually step three feet.

6. After all the arrangements are made, the seconds determine the giving of the word and position, by lot; and he who gains has the choice of the one or the other, selects whether it be the word or the position, but he cannot have both.

CHAPTER IV. Duty of Challengee and Second After Challenge Sent.

1. The challengee has no option when negotiation has ceased, but to accept the challenge.

2. The second makes the necessary arrangements with the second of the person challenging. The arrangements are detailed in the preceding chapter.

CHAPTER V. Duty of Principals and Seconds on the Ground.

1. The principals are to be respectful in meeting, and neither by look or expression irritate each other. They are to be wholly passive, being entirely under the guidance of their seconds.

2. When once posted, they are not to quit their positions under any circumstances, without leave or direction of their seconds.

3. When the principals are posted, the second giving the word, must tell them to stand firm until he repeats the giving of the word, in the manner it will be given when the parties are at liberty to fire.

4. Each second has a loaded pistol, in order to enforce a fair combat according to the rules agreed on; and if a principal fires before the word or time agreed on, he is at liberty to fire at him, and if such second's principal fall, it is his duty to do so.

5. If after a fire, either party be touched, the duel is to end; and no second is excusable who permits a wounded friend to fight; and no second who knows his duty, will permit his friend to fight a man already hit. I am aware there have been many instances where a contest has continued, not only after slight, but severe wounds, had been received. In all such cases, I think the seconds are blamable.

6. If after an exchange of shots, neither party be hit, it is the duty of the second of the challengee, to approach the second of the challenger and say: "Our friends have exchanged shots, are you satisfied, or is there any cause why the contest should be continued?" If the meeting be of no serious cause of complaint, where the party

complaining had in no way been deeply injured, or grossly insulted, the second of the party challenging should reply: "The point of honor being settled, there can, I conceive, be no objection to a reconciliation, and I propose that our principals meet on middle ground, shake hands, and be friends." If this be acceded to by the second of the challengee, the second of the party challenging, says: "We have agreed that the present duel shall cease, the honor of each of you is preserved, and you will meet on middle ground, shake hands and be reconciled."

7. If the insult be of a serious character, it will be the duty of the second of the challenger, to say, in reply to the second of the challengee: "We have been deeply wronged, and if you are not disposed to repair the injury, the contest must continue." And if the challengee offers nothing by way of reparation, the fight continues until one or the other of the principals is hit.

8. If in cases where the contest is ended by the seconds, as mentioned in the sixth rule of this chapter, the parties refuse to meet and be reconciled, it is the duty of the seconds to withdraw from the field, informing their principals, that the contest must be continued under the superintendence of other friends. But if one agrees to this arrangement of the seconds, and the other does not, the second of the disagreeing principal only withdraws.

9. If either principal on the ground refuses to fight or continue the fight when required, it is the duty of his second to say to the other second: "I have come upon the ground with a coward, and do tender you my apology for an ignorance of his character; you are at liberty to post him." The second, by such conduct, stands excused to the opposite party.

10. When the duel is ended by a party being hit, it is the duty of the second to the party so hit, to announce the fact to the second of the party hitting, who will forthwith tender any assistance he can command

to the disabled principal. If the party challenging, hit the challengee, it is his duty to say he is satisfied, and will leave the ground. If the challenger be hit, upon the challengee being informed of it, he should ask through his second, whether he is at liberty to leave the ground which should be assented to.

CHAPTER VI. Who Should Be on the Ground.

1. The principals, seconds, one surgeon and one assistant surgeon to each principal; but the assistant surgeon may be dispensed with.

2. Any number of friends that the seconds agree on, may be present, provided they do not come within the degrees of consanguinity mentioned in the seventh rule of Chapter I. 3. Persons admitted on the ground, are carefully to abstain by word or behavior, from any act that might be the least exceptionable; nor should they stand near the principals or seconds, or hold conversations with them.

CHAPTER VII. Arms, and Manner of Loading and Presenting Them.

1. The arms used should be smooth-bore pistols, not exceeding nine inches in length, with flint and steel. Percussion pistols may be mutually used if agreed on, but to object on that account is lawful.

2. Each second informs the other when he is about to load, and invites

his presence, but the seconds rarely attend on such invitation, as gentlemen may be safely trusted in the matter.

3. The second, in presenting the pistol to his friend, should never put it in his pistol hand, but should place it in the other, which is grasped midway the barrel, with muzzle pointing in the contrary way to that which he is to fire, informing him that his pistol is loaded and ready for use. Before the word is given, the principal grasps the butt firmly in his pistol hand, and brings it round, with the muzzle downward, to the fighting position.

4. The fighting position, is with the muzzle down and the barrel from you; for although it may be agreed that you may hold your pistol with the muzzle up, it may be objected to, as you can fire sooner from that position, and consequently have a decided advantage, which ought not to be claimed, and should not be granted.

CHAPTER VIII. The Degrees of Insult, and How Compromised

1. The prevailing rule is, that words used in retort, although more violent and disrespectful than those first used, will not satisfy,--words being no satisfaction for words.

2. When words are used, and a blow given in return, the insult is avenged; and if redress be sought, it must be from the person receiving the blow.

3. When blows are given in the first instance and not returned, and the

person first striking, be badly beaten or otherwise, the party first struck is to make the demand, for blows do not satisfy a blow.

4. Insults at a wine table, when the company are over-excited, must be answered for; and if the party insulting have no recollection of the insult, it is his duty to say so in writing, and negative the insult. For instance, if the man say: "you are a liar and no gentleman," he must, in addition to the plea of the want of recollection, say: "I believe the party insulted to be a man of the strictest veracity and a gentleman."

5. Intoxication is not a full excuse for insult, but it will greatly palliate. If it was a full excuse, it might be well counterfeited to wound feelings, or destroy character.

6. In all cases of intoxication, the seconds must use a sound discretion under the above general rules.

7. Can every insult be compromised? is a mooted and vexed question. On this subject, no rules can be given that will be satisfactory. The old opinion, that a blow must require blood, is not of force. Blows may be compromised in many cases. What those are, much depend on the seconds.

APPENDIX.

Since the above Code was in press, a friend has favored me with the IRISH CODE OF HONOR, which I had never seen; and it is published as an Appendix to it. One thing must be apparent to every reader, viz., the marked amelioration of the rules that govern in duelling at the present time. I am unable to say what code exists now in

Ireland, but I very much doubt whether it be of the same character which it bore in 1777. The American Quarterly Review for September, 1824, in a notice of Sir Jonah Barrington's history of his own times, has published this code; and followed it up with some remarks, which I have thought proper to insert also. The grave reviewer has spoken of certain States in terms so unlike a gentleman, that I would advise him to look at home, and say whether he does not think that the manners of his own countrymen, do not require great amendment? I am very sure, that the citizens of the States so disrespectfully spoken of, would feel a deep humiliation, to be compelled to exchange their urbanity of deportment, for the uncouth incivility of the people of Massachusetts. Look at their public journals, and you will find them, very generally, teeming with abuse of private character, which would not be countenanced here. The idea of New England becoming a school for manners, is about as fanciful as Bolinbroke's "idea of a patriot king." I like their fortiter in re, but utterly eschew their suaviter in modo.

"The practice of duelling and points of honor settled at Clonmell summer assizes, 1777, by the gentleman delegates of Tipperary, Galway, Mayo, Sligo and Roscommon, and prescribed for general adoption throughout Ireland.

"Rule 1.--The first offence requires the apology, although the retort may have been more offensive than the insult.--Example: A. tells B. he is impertinent, &C.; B. retorts, that he lies; yet A. must make the first apology, because he gave the first offence, and then, (after one fire,) B. may explain away the retort by subsequent apology.

"Rule 2.--But if the parties would rather fight on: then, after two shots each, (but in no case before,) B. may explain first, and A. apologize afterward.

"Rule 3.--If a doubt exist who gave the first offence, the decision rests with the seconds; if they won't decide or can't agree, the matter must proceed to two shots, or a hit, if the challenger requires it.

"Rule 4.--When the lie direct is the first offence, the aggressor must either beg pardon in express terms; exchange tow shots previous to apology; or three shots followed up by explanation; or fire on till a severe hit be received by one party or the other.

"Rule 5.--As a blow is strictly prohibited under any circumstances among gentlemen, no verbal apology can be received for such an insult; the alternatives therefore are: the offender handing a can to the injured party, to be used on his own back, at the same time begging pardon; firing on until one or both is disabled; or exchanging three shots, and then asking pardon without the proffer of the cane.

"If swords are used, the parties engage till one is well-blooded, disabled or disarmed; or until, after receiving a wound, and blood being drawn, the aggressor begs pardon.

"N.B. A disarm is considered the same as a disable; the disarmer may (strictly) break his adversary's sword; but if it be the challenger who is disarmed, it is considered ungenerous to do so.

"In case the challenged be disarmed and refuses to ask pardon or atone, he must not be killed as formerly; but the challenger may lay his sword on the aggressor's shoulder, than break the aggressor's sword, and say, 'I spare your life!' The challenged can never revive the quarrel, the challenger may.

"Rule 6.--If A. give B. the lie, and B. retorts by a blow, (being the two greatest offences,) no reconciliation can take place till after two discharges each, or a severe hit; after which, B. may beg A.'s pardon for the blow, and then A. may explain simply for the lie; because a blow is never allowable, and the offence of the lie therefore merges in it. (See preceding rule.)

"N.B. Challenges for individual causes, may be reconciled on the ground, after one shot. An explanation, or the slightest hit should be sufficient in such cases, because no personal offence transpired.

"Rule 7.--But no apology can be received, in any case, after the parties have actually taken their ground, without exchange of fires.

"Rule 8.--In the above case, no challenger is obliged to divulge the cause of his challenge, (if private,) unless required by the challenged to do so before their meeting.

"Rule 9.--All imputations of cheating at play, races, &c, to be considered equivalent to a blow; but may be reconciled after one shot, on admitting their falsehood, and begging pardon publicly.

"Rule 10.--Any insult to a lady under a gentleman's care or protection, to be considered as, by one degree, a greater offence than if given to the gentleman personally, and to be regulated accordingly.

"Rule 11.--Offences originating or accruing from the support of a lady's reputation, to be considered as less unjustifiable than any other of the same class, and as admitting of lighter apologies by the aggressor; this to be determined by the circumstances of the case, but always favorably to the lady.

"Rule 12.--In simple unpremeditated rencontres with the small sword or couteau-de-chasse, the rule is, first draw, first sheathe; unless blood be drawn: then both sheathe, and proceed to investigation.

"Rule 13.--No dumb-shooting, or firing in the air, admissible in any case. The challenger ought not to have challenged without receiving offence; and the challenged ought, if he gave offence, to have made an apology before he came on the ground: therefore, children's play must be dishonorable on one side or the other, and is accordingly prohibited.

"Rule 14.--Seconds to be of equal rank in society with the principals they attend, inasmuch as a second may choose or chance to become a principal, and equality is indispensable.

"Rule 15.--Challenges are never to be delivered at night, unless the party to be challenged intend leaving the place of offence before morning; for it is desirable to avoid all hot-headed proceedings.

"Rule 16.--The challenged has the right to choose his own weapon, unless the challenger gives his honor he is no swordsman; after which, however, he cannot decline any second species of weapon proposed by the challenged.

"Rule 17.--The challenged chooses his ground; the challenger chooses his distance; the seconds fix the time and terms of firing.

"Rule 18.--The seconds load in presence of each other, unless they give their mutual honors that they have charged smooth and single, which should be held sufficient.

"Rule 19.--Firing may be regulated, first by signal; secondly, by word of command; or, thirdly, at pleasure, as may be agreeable to the parties. In the latter case, the parties may fire at their reasonable leisure, but second presents and rests are strictly prohibited.

"Rule 20.--In all cases a miss-fire is equivalent to a shot, and a snap or a non-cock is to be considered as a miss-fire.

"Rule 21.--Seconds are bound to attempt a reconciliation before the meeting takes place, or after sufficient firing or hits, as specified.

"Rule 22.--Any wound sufficient to agitate the nerves and necessarily make the hands shake, must end the business for that day.

"Rule 23.--If the cause of meeting be of such a nature that no apology or explanation can or will be received, the challenged takes his ground, and calls on the challenger to proceed as he chooses: in such cases firing at pleasure is the usual practice, but may be varied by agreement.

"Rule 24.--In slight cases, the second hands his principal but one pistol; but in gross cases, two, holding another case ready charged in reserve.

"Rule 25.--When seconds disagree, and resolve to exchange shots themselves, it must be at the same time and at right angles with their principals.

"If with swords, side by side, at five paces interval.

"N.B. All matters and doubts not herein mentioned, will be explained and cleared up by application to the committee, who meet alternately at Clonmell and Galway, at their quarter sessions, for the purpose.

    "CROW RYAN, President."

    "JAMES KEOG,
    "AMBY BODKIN, Secretaries."

ADDITIONAL GALWAY ARTICLES

"Rule 1.--No party can be allowed to bend his knee or cover his side with his left hand; but may present at any level from the hip to the eye.

"Rule 2.--One can neither advance nor retreat, if the ground be measured. If the ground be unmeasured, either party may advance at pleasure, even to touch muzzle; but neither can advance on his adversary after the fire, unless his adversary step forward on him.

"The seconds stand responsible for this last rule being strictly observed; bad cases have accrued from neglecting it."

This precise and enlightened digest was rendered necessary by the multitude of quarrels that arouse without "sufficient dignified provocation:" the point of honor men required a uniform government; and the code thus formed was disseminated throughout the island, with directions that it should be strictly observed by all gentlemen, and kept in their pistol cases. The rules, with some others, were commonly styled "the thirty-six commandments," and, according to the author, have been much acted upon down to the present day. Tipperary and Galway were the chief schools of duelling. We remember to have heard, in travelling to the town of the former name in a stage coach, a dispute between two Irish companions, on the point, which was the most gentlemanly country in all Ireland--Tipperary or Galway? and both laid great stress upon the relative duelling merits of those counties. By the same criterion, Tennessee, Kentucky, Georgia and South Carolina, would bear away the palm of gentility among the States of the Union.

The Codes Of Hammurabi And Moses
W. W. Davies

QTY

The discovery of the Hammurabi Code is one of the greatest achievements of archaeology, and is of paramount interest, not only to the student of the Bible, but also to all those interested in ancient history...

Religion   ISBN: *1-59462-338-4*   Pages:132
MSRP *$12.95*

The Theory of Moral Sentiments
Adam Smith

QTY

This work from 1749. contains original theories of conscience amd moral judgment and it is the foundation for systemof morals.

Philosophy   ISBN: *1-59462-777-0*   Pages:536
MSRP *$19.95*

Jessica's First Prayer
Hesba Stretton

QTY

In a screened and secluded corner of one of the many railway-bridges which span the streets of London there could be seen a few years ago, from five o'clock every morning until half past eight, a tidily set-out coffee-stall, consisting of a trestle and board, upon which stood two large tin cans, with a small fire of charcoal burning under each so as to keep the coffee boiling during the early hours of the morning when the work-people were thronging into the city on their way to their daily toil...

Childrens   ISBN: *1-59462-373-2*   Pages:84
MSRP *$9.95*

My Life and Work
Henry Ford

QTY

Henry Ford revolutionized the world with his implementation of mass production for the Model T automobile. Gain valuable business insight into his life and work with his own auto-biography... "We have only started on our development of our country we have not as yet, with all our talk of wonderful progress, done more than scratch the surface. The progress has been wonderful enough but..."

Biographies/   ISBN: *1-59462-198-5*   Pages:300
MSRP *$21.95*

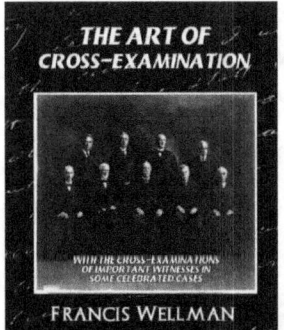

The Art of Cross-Examination
Francis Wellman

QTY

I presume it is the experience of every author, after his first book is published upon an important subject, to be almost overwhelmed with a wealth of ideas and illustrations which could readily have been included in his book, and which to his own mind, at least, seem to make a second edition inevitable. Such certainly was the case with me; and when the first edition had reached its sixth impression in five months, I rejoiced to learn that it seemed to my publishers that the book had met with a sufficiently favorable reception to justify a second and considerably enlarged edition. ..

Pages:412

Reference   **ISBN:** *1-59462-647-2*   *MSRP $19.95*

On the Duty of Civil Disobedience
Henry David Thoreau

QTY

Thoreau wrote his famous essay, On the Duty of Civil Disobedience, as a protest against an unjust but popular war and the immoral but popular institution of slave-owning. He did more than write—he declined to pay his taxes, and was hauled off to gaol in consequence. Who can say how much this refusal of his hastened the end of the war and of slavery ?

Law   **ISBN:** *1-59462-747-9*   **Pages:48**

MSRP $7.45

Dream Psychology Psychoanalysis for Beginners
Sigmund Freud

QTY

Sigmund Freud, born Sigismund Schlomo Freud (May 6, 1856 - September 23, 1939), was a Jewish-Austrian neurologist and psychiatrist who co-founded the psychoanalytic school of psychology. Freud is best known for his theories of the unconscious mind, especially involving the mechanism of repression; his redefinition of sexual desire as mobile and directed towards a wide variety of objects; and his therapeutic techniques, especially his understanding of transference in the therapeutic relationship and the presumed value of dreams as sources of insight into unconscious desires.

Pages:196

Psychology   **ISBN:** *1-59462-905-6*   *MSRP $15.45*

The Miracle of Right Thought
Orison Swett Marden

QTY

Believe with all of your heart that you will do what you were made to do. When the mind has once formed the habit of holding cheerful, happy, prosperous pictures, it will not be easy to form the opposite habit. It does not matter how improbable or how far away this realization may see, or how dark the prospects may be, if we visualize them as best we can, as vividly as possible, hold tenaciously to them and vigorously struggle to attain them, they will gradually become actualized, realized in the life. But a desire, a longing without endeavor, a yearning abandoned or held indifferently will vanish without realization.

Pages:360

Self Help   **ISBN:** *1-59462-644-8*   *MSRP $25.45*

QTY

The Rosicrucian Cosmo-Conception Mystic Christianity *by Max Heindel*　　ISBN: *1-59462-188-8*　**$38.95**
The Rosicrucian Cosmo-conception is not dogmatic, neither does it appeal to any other authority than the reason of the student. It is: not controversial, but is: sent forth in the, hope that it may help to clear...　　　New Age/Religion Pages 646

Abandonment To Divine Providence *by Jean-Pierre de Caussade*　　ISBN: *1-59462-228-0*　**$25.95**
"The Rev. Jean Pierre de Caussade was one of the most remarkable spiritual writers of the Society of Jesus in France in the 18th Century. His death took place at Toulouse in 1751. His works have gone through many editions and have been republished...　　Inspirational/Religion Pages 400

Mental Chemistry *by Charles Haanel*　　ISBN: *1-59462-192-6*　**$23.95**
Mental Chemistry allows the change of material conditions by combining and appropriately utilizing the power of the mind. Much like applied chemistry creates something new and unique out of careful combinations of chemicals the mastery of mental chemistry...　　New Age Pages 354

The Letters of Robert Browning and Elizabeth Barret Barrett 1845-1846 vol II　　ISBN: *1-59462-193-4*　**$35.95**
by Robert Browning and Elizabeth Barrett　　Biographies Pages 596

Gleanings In Genesis (volume I) *by Arthur W. Pink*　　ISBN: *1-59462-130-6*　**$27.45**
Appropriately has Genesis been termed "the seed plot of the Bible" for in it we have, in germ form, almost all of the great doctrines which are afterwards fully developed in the books of Scripture which follow...　　Religion/Inspirational Pages 420

The Master Key *by L. W. de Laurence*　　ISBN: *1-59462-001-6*　**$30.95**
In no branch of human knowledge has there been a more lively increase of the spirit of research during the past few years than in the study of Psychology, Concentration and Mental Discipline. The requests for authentic lessons in Thought Control, Mental Discipline and...　　New Age/Business Pages 422

The Lesser Key Of Solomon Goetia *by L. W. de Laurence*　　ISBN: *1-59462-092-X*　**$9.95**
This translation of the first book of the "Lernegton" which is now for the first time made accessible to students of Talismanic Magic was done, after careful collation and edition, from numerous Ancient Manuscripts in Hebrew, Latin, and French...　　New Age/Occult Pages 92

Rubaiyat Of Omar Khayyam *by Edward Fitzgerald*　　ISBN:*1-59462-332-5*　**$13.95**
Edward Fitzgerald, whom the world has already learned, in spite of his own efforts to remain within the shadow of anonymity, to look upon as one of the rarest poets of the century, was born at Bredfield, in Suffolk, on the 31st of March, 1809. He was the third son of John Purcell...　　Music Pages 172

Ancient Law *by Henry Maine*　　ISBN: *1-59462-128-4*　**$29.95**
The chief object of the following pages is to indicate some of the earliest ideas of mankind, as they are reflected in Ancient Law, and to point out the relation of those ideas to modern thought.　　Religion/History Pages 452

Far-Away Stories *by William J. Locke*　　ISBN: *1-59462-129-2*　**$19.45**
"Good wine needs no bush, but a collection of mixed vintages does. And this book is just such a collection. Some of the stories I do not want to remain buried for ever in the museum files of dead magazine-numbers an author's not unpardonable vanity..."　　Fiction Pages 272

Life of David Crockett *by David Crockett*　　ISBN: *1-59462-250-7*　**$27.45**
"Colonel David Crockett was one of the most remarkable men of the times in which he lived. Born in humble life, but gifted with a strong will, an indomitable courage, and unremitting perseverance...　　Biographies/New Age Pages 424

Lip-Reading *by Edward Nitchie*　　ISBN: *1-59462-206-X*　**$25.95**
Edward B. Nitchie, founder of the New York School for the Hard of Hearing, now the Nitchie School of Lip-Reading, Inc, wrote "LIP-READING Principles and Practice". The development and perfecting of this meritorious work on lip-reading was an undertaking...　　How-to Pages 400

A Handbook of Suggestive Therapeutics, Applied Hypnotism, Psychic Science　　ISBN: *1-59462-214-0*　**$24.95**
by Henry Munro　　Health/New Age/Health/Self-help Pages 376

A Doll's House: and Two Other Plays *by Henrik Ibsen*　　ISBN: *1-59462-112-8*　**$19.95**
Henrik Ibsen created this classic when in revolutionary 1848 Rome. Introducing some striking concepts in playwriting for the realist genre, this play has been studied the world over.　　Fiction/Classics/Plays 308

The Light of Asia *by sir Edwin Arnold*　　ISBN: *1-59462-204-3*　**$13.95**
In this poetic masterpiece, Edwin Arnold describes the life and teachings of Buddha. The man who was to become known as Buddha to the world was born as Prince Gautama of India but he rejected the worldly riches and abandoned the reigns of power when...　　Religion/History/Biographies Pages 170

The Complete Works of Guy de Maupassant *by Guy de Maupassant*　　ISBN: *1-59462-157-8*　**$16.95**
"For days and days, nights and nights, I had dreamed of that first kiss which was to consecrate our engagement, and I knew not on what spot I should put my lips..."　　Fiction/Classics Pages 240

The Art of Cross-Examination *by Francis L. Wellman*　　ISBN: *1-59462-309-0*　**$26.95**
Written by a renowned trial lawyer, Wellman imparts his experience and uses case studies to explain how to use psychology to extract desired information through questioning.　　How-to/Science/Reference Pages 408

Answered or Unanswered? *by Louisa Vaughan*　　ISBN: *1-59462-248-5*　**$10.95**
Miracles of Faith in China　　Religion Pages 112

The Edinburgh Lectures on Mental Science (1909) *by Thomas*　　ISBN: *1-59462-008-3*　**$11.95**
This book contains the substance of a course of lectures recently given by the writer in the Queen Street Hall, Edinburgh. Its purpose is to indicate the Natural Principles governing the relation between Mental Action and Material Conditions...　　New Age/Psychology Pages 148

Ayesha *by H. Rider Haggard*　　ISBN: *1-59462-301-5*　**$24.95**
Verily and indeed it is the unexpected that happens! Probably if there was one person upon the earth from whom the Editor of this, and of a certain previous history, did not expect to hear again...　　Classics Pages 380

Ayala's Angel *by Anthony Trollope*　　ISBN: *1-59462-352-X*　**$29.95**
The two girls were both pretty, but Lucy who was twenty-one who supposed to be simple and comparatively unattractive, whereas Ayala was credited, as her Bombwhat romantic name might show, with poetic charm and a taste for romance. Ayala when her father died was nineteen...　　Fiction Pages 484

The American Commonwealth *by James Bryce*　　ISBN: *1-59462-286-8*　**$34.45**
An interpretation of American democratic political theory. It examines political mechanics and society from the perspective of Scotsman James Bryce　　Politics Pages 572

Stories of the Pilgrims *by Margaret P. Pumphrey*　　ISBN: *1-59462-116-0*　**$17.95**
This book explores pilgrims religious oppression in England as well as their escape to Holland and eventual crossing to America on the Mayflower, and their early days in New England...　　History Pages 268

QTY

The Fasting Cure *by Sinclair Upton* ISBN: *1-59462-222-1* **$13.95**
In the Cosmopolitan Magazine for May, 1910, and in the Contemporary Review (London) for April, 1910, I published an article dealing with my experiences in fasting. I have written a great many magazine articles, but never one which attracted so much attention... New Age/Self Help/Health Pages 164

Hebrew Astrology *by Sepharial* ISBN: *1-59462-308-2* **$13.45**
In these days of advanced thinking it is a matter of common observation that we have left many of the old landmarks behind and that we are now pressing forward to greater heights and to a wider horizon than that which represented the mind-content of our progenitors... Astrology Pages 144

Thought Vibration or The Law of Attraction in the Thought World ISBN: *1-59462-127-6* **$12.95**
by William Walker Atkinson *Psychology/Religion Pages 144*

Optimism *by Helen Keller* ISBN: *1-59462-108-X* **$15.95**
Helen Keller was blind, deaf, and mute since 19 months old, yet famously learned how to overcome these handicaps, communicate with the world, and spread her lectures promoting optimism. An inspiring read for everyone... Biographies/Inspirational Pages 84

Sara Crewe *by Frances Burnett* ISBN: *1-59462-360-0* **$9.45**
In the first place, Miss Minchin lived in London. Her home was a large, dull, tall one, in a large, dull square, where all the houses were alike, and all the sparrows were alike, and where all the door-knockers made the same heavy sound... Childrens/Classic Pages 88

The Autobiography of Benjamin Franklin *by Benjamin Franklin* ISBN: *1-59462-135-7* **$24.95**
The Autobiography of Benjamin Franklin has probably been more extensively read than any other American historical work, and no other book of its kind has had such ups and downs of fortune. Franklin lived for many years in England, where he was agent... Biographies/History Pages 332

Name	
Email	
Telephone	
Address	
City, State ZIP	

☐ **Credit Card**   ☐ **Check / Money Order**

Credit Card Number	
Expiration Date	
Signature	

Please Mail to: Book Jungle
PO Box 2226
Champaign, IL 61825
or Fax to: 630-214-0564

ORDERING INFORMATION

web: *www.bookjungle.com*
email: *sales@bookjungle.com*
fax: *630-214-0564*
mail: *Book Jungle PO Box 2226 Champaign, IL 61825*
or PayPal *to sales@bookjungle.com*

Please contact us for bulk discounts

DIRECT-ORDER TERMS

20% Discount if You Order Two or More Books
Free Domestic Shipping!
Accepted: Master Card, Visa, Discover, American Express

www.ingramcontent.com/pod-product-compliance
Lightning Source LLC
Chambersburg PA
CBHW082018170626
46817CB00009B/3134